Patricia Coombs

Dorrie and the Amazing Magic Elixir

Lothrop, Lee & Shepard Co. / New York

Other books by Patricia Coombs

Dorrie and the Birthday Eggs
Dorrie and the Blue Witch
Dorrie and the Fortune Teller
Dorrie and the Goblin
Dorrie and the Haunted House
Dorrie and the Weather-Box
Dorrie and the Witch Doctor
Dorrie and the Wizard's Spell
Lisa and the Grompet
Mouse Café

Copyright © 1974 by Patricia Coombs.
All rights reserved. No part of this book may be reproduced or utilized in any form or by any means, electronic or mechanical, including photocopying, recording or by any information retrieval system, without permission in writing from the Publisher. Inquiries should be addressed to Lothrop, Lee and Shepard Company, 105 Madison Ave., New York, N.Y. 10016. Printed in the United States of America.
1 2 3 4 5 78 77 76 75 74

Library of Congress Cataloging in Publication Data

Coombs, Patricia.
   Dorrie and the amazing magic elixir.

   SUMMARY: Left in charge of an elixir that will make one spell-proof, Dorrie, the little witch, foils the Green Wizard's attempt to steal it.
   [1. Witches—Fiction] I. Title.
PZ7.C7813Dg   [Fic]   74-4206
ISBN 0-688-41640-3
ISBN 0-688-51640-8 (lib. bdg.)

LARA DIANE

TONYA SUE

AND

PAMELA MARIE

COOMBS

This is Dorrie. She is a witch. A little witch. Her hat is always on crooked. Her socks never match. She lives with her mother, the Big Witch, and Cook and her black cat, Gink.

One dark Thursday the Big Witch was in her secret room at the top of the tower. She was mixing up magic.

Dorrie and Gink sat on the stairs outside the door. They listened to the magic sounds, the bubbling and stirring and chanting. Bright sparks of magic floated and melted in the air around them.

"Gink," whispered Dorrie, "Mother has been working for weeks on a new recipe. I don't think it's ever going to turn out right. I wish we could help."

Clouds of magic steam floated down. There was a popping sound. The chanting stopped. The door at the top of the tower flew open.

"Eureka! A new recipe!
A marvelous discovery!
A MAGIC ELIXIR!"
cried the Big Witch.

Dorrie and Gink ran into the secret room to look. Colors swirled and shimmered over the Big Witch's cauldron. Inside the cauldron was a smaller cauldron. Inside that cauldron was a bowl. Inside the bowl was a jar. Inside the jar was the Magic Elixir.

"Wow!" said Dorrie. "If such a little bit took so long to make, it must be awfully strong stuff."

"It will be even stronger," said the Big Witch, "when it is done. I used up all the moon herbs and I have to gather more before dark. The Magic Elixir must simmer and stay warm until the moon herbs are added. Cook will have to take care of it while I'm gone."

"It's Thursday," said Dorrie. "Cook's gone to the dentist."

"Oh, no!" cried the Big Witch. "What will I do? If I don't gather the moon herbs before dark, I'll have to wait until after the next full moon. The Magic Elixir will be spoiled!"

"I can take care of the Magic Elixir," said Dorrie. "I'll keep it warm. I'll do just what you tell me to do."

"Well, let me think," said the Big Witch. "I know! I'll stop at Mr. Obs's house on the way. He's always home on Thursday. He'd be glad to help."

"Oh, good, I'd like that," said Dorrie happily.

The Big Witch showed Dorrie how to stir the Magic Elixir, slowly, seven times every seven minutes. She showed Dorrie how to use the timer and how to keep the magic flame under the cauldron just an inch high.

Dorrie and the Big Witch were so busy they didn't see a greenish face slide up against the tower window. They didn't know a greenish ear was listening to every word.

"I'll make one test before I go," said the Big Witch. "So you can see what an amazing discovery it is."

The Big Witch put a dab of Magic Elixir on a pair of glasses. She dropped them on the floor. She jumped up and down on them. They didn't bend or crack or break.

"It makes things *indestructible,*" said the Big Witch. "And most amazing of all, it makes people *hex-proof, spell-proof, potion-proof!* When more moon herbs are added, the Magic Elixir will be twice as strong. Just one drop will protect a person from hexes, spells, potions. Just think, when it is done there will be enough in this little jar to save all our friends from evil spells, forever! Now I must fly!"

Dorrie went downstairs with the Big Witch to say goodbye. Greenish eyes watched them leave the secret room. Greenish fingers slid into the crack beside the window, testing the latch.

"Hex-proof, spell-proof, potion-proof, and *indestructible!* What luck!" Greenish teeth gleamed. "I'll be safe from spells forever! Even the Big Witch's nasty spells will roll off me like rain off a bat. Now, to pry this window open and get inside before that witch-brat gets back. If she sees me and nails the window shut, my plot is wrecked!"

Downstairs the Big Witch put on her cloak and got out her broomstick. "Lock the door as soon as I leave. Don't let anyone in except Mr. Obs. Not until you hear my special knock."

"Don't worry, Mother," said Dorrie. "I'll be careful. And nobody knows about the Magic Elixir anyway."

Away over the treetops flew the Big Witch, and down toward Mr. Obs's house. Dorrie closed the door and locked it.

"Come on, Gink, we've got a very important job to do."

Up, up, up the stairs they went. Up, up, up the dark stairs to the secret room.

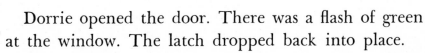

Dorrie opened the door. There was a flash of green at the window. The latch dropped back into place.

Dorrie blinked. "I'm seeing things. It must have been sparks from the magic."

Dorrie got to work. First she opened the Big Witch's closet. She took out a big black apron and put it on. She turned the timer. And she stirred the Magic Elixir, slowly, seven times. She made sure the flame under the cauldron was just an inch high. She climbed up on the stool to watch the Magic Elixir simmer.

All at once there was a loud knocking downstairs.

"Come on, Gink, Mr. Obs is here!" said Dorrie, jumping down from the stool.

Down, down, down the stairs they went. The knocking had stopped. Dorrie went to the door. She looked out. Mr. Obs wasn't there. Nobody was there. Just some greenish mist melting in the air.

"That's funny," said Dorrie. She ran into the kitchen and looked out the back door. Nobody was there either. And the yard was empty.

Back up the stairs they went, and up, up, up into the tower. Dorrie opened the door to the secret room and hurried inside.

"Oh, bother," cried Dorrie. "The window blew open. The magic flame is out!"

Dorrie pulled the window shut. She rushed back to the cauldron to fix the flame. When it was just an inch high again, she turned the timer. Then she stirred the Magic Elixir seven times.

"Phew," said Dorrie, patting Gink, "that was close. The Magic Elixir nearly got spoiled while we were downstairs. I wish Mr. Obs would hurry!"

Outside the tower window, greenish fingers slid through the crack toward the latch again.

The secret room grew darker as it grew later. And still Mr. Obs didn't come. Dorrie bent over the Magic Elixir, counting and stirring. The colors shimmered and simmered and glowed. In the shadows over the table hung cages of bats and lizards and owls.

All at once there was a knocking downstairs. It got louder and louder.

"Mr. Obs is here at last! Come on, Gink," cried Dorrie. And down, down, down the dark stairs they went. They ran to the front door. The knocking had stopped. Dorrie looked out. Mr. Obs wasn't there. Just a flash of green. Dorrie blinked and looked again.

No one was there. Dorrie looked out the windows. She looked out the kitchen door. No one was there either. The yard was empty.

"Hmph," said Dorrie. "Mr. Obs is *never* late. He always comes right over. Oh, oh, it's time to stir the Magic Elixir!"

Dorrie ran back up the stairs.

Gink went with her.

Up, up, up into the tower they ran. Dorrie flung open the door, just as a green shape flashed from the window into the shadows of the Big Witch's closet.

"That dumb window blew open *again!*" said Dorrie crossly. She slammed it shut and ran to the cauldron.

First she fixed the flame. She turned the timer. Then she stirred slowly seven times.

Behind her the closet door slowly opened. Green eyes peered at the Magic Elixir, and at Dorrie. Green toes began creeping up behind Dorrie. Green fingers reached into a pouch. A green hand full of magic powder reached toward Dorrie.

Just then Dorrie sneezed. She stepped back. She landed smack on the green toes.

There was an awful yell. Dorrie jumped. Gink hissed. Bottles of magic fell. The spoon went flying.

"OW! OW! OW! My toes, my toes! You've bent my toes, you witch-brat! EEEEE-OW!"

Dorrie stamped her foot. "Stop that racket! What are you doing sneaking around our tower? Who are you?"

"The Green Wizard!" he snarled. "I'm here to get my revenge on the Big Witch. She cast a spell on me, and for twenty years I've been a hat rack in a witches' tearoom. ME, the most famous thief and spy who ever flew a broomstick. Now I've got her where I want her. Once I've drunk up that Magic Elixir, she'll be powerless. Every witch in the world will be powerless against me! I'll be spell-proof, hex-proof, potion-proof, and INDESTRUCTIBLE!"

"Hmph!" said Dorrie. "You can't outsmart the Big Witch. She'll turn you into a pot holder in two seconds flat."

"Ha! Not if I get that Magic Elixir before she gets home," snarled the Green Wizard. "Out of my way!" He gave Dorrie a shove and kicked Gink away. "Cats! Witches! Yuck!"

Dorrie grabbed a bottle of magic and swung it at him. "Get away from this Magic Elixir!" yelled Dorrie. "And leave my cat alone! Mr. Obs will be here any second. Then you'll be sorry."

The Green Wizard hissed through his teeth. He reached into his pocket. He tossed something on the table beside Dorrie. "He's already here!" laughed the Wizard.

Dorrie looked. There was a round brown toad on the table. And something about it looked familiar. The toad clasped its fingers together. It looked at Dorrie with tears in its eyes.

"Mr. Obs!" gasped Dorrie. "It's you!"

The toad nodded. Dorrie spun around and glared at the Green Wizard. "No wonder my mother put you under a spell. You're a really mean and rotten wizard!"

"Out of my way, you pesky pest. That Elixir is going to be mine, all mine!" yelled the Wizard.

Mr. Obs croaked a warning. But it was too late. There was a flash of green. Powder from .the Wizard's pouch covered Dorrie from head to toe.

"Oh, oh!" cried Dorrie. She felt herself whirling down, growing smaller and smaller and smaller. Her socks were bending underneath her and changing color. Her fingers and toes grew long and bumpy.

"I'm a toad! I'm a toad, too! Mr. Obs, what are we going to do? Somehow we have to keep the Green Wizard from drinking the Magic Elixir. If he drinks it before Mother gets home, he'll be indestructible. She won't be able to do anything!"

Crouched together they watched the Green Wizard. He rubbed his hands together, gazing greedily into the Big Witch's cauldron. He blew out the magic flame. He began to fan the cauldron with his hat to cool it off.

Dorrie frowned. She hopped over to the cauldron and stamped her toad feet at the Green Wizard. "Don't let the Elixir get cold. It isn't done yet. It has to stay warm!"

The Green Wizard scowled at Dorrie. "Don't try to fool me. It's cooked long enough to work on one person and I'm going to *drink it all*. All I have to do is get it cool enough to swallow before the Big Witch comes back. Get away, you lumpy creep, or I'll dump you and your friend right out the window." He gave the table a loud whack with his green fist.

Mr. Obs was so scared he leaped into the air. He landed inside an empty jar.

"Help, I've been thrown in prison!" croaked Mr. Obs.

"Oh, my," croaked Dorrie. "Things are not going at all well."

"Stop that croaking over there!" screeched the Green Wizard.

Dorrie and Mr. Obs stopped talking and watched. The secret room grew darker and darker. The Green Wizard was blowing on the cauldron to cool it off. The only light was the glowing cauldron and the fading showers of sparks above it.

Dorrie sighed. She looked at Mr. Obs's sad round shape in the jar. She looked down at her own toad fingers. Her round eyes grew rounder.

"Mother's *Book of Magic*," whispered Dorrie. "I'm sitting right on it and I can still read! I'm still me even if I am a toad. That means I can work a spell. But I've got to hurry if I'm going to keep the Green Wizard from drinking the Elixir."

Dorrie hopped around the pages. "Ah ha!" she croaked, "this will do it!" With clumsy jumps she hopped in a circle three times, croaking:

Abacadabra turn me, turn,
Turn me once and twice and thrice,
Magic jumps and magic cries
Turn me back to my own size,
Toadleywoadleynoadleyknee!

Dorrie closed her eyes and turned on her toes. She counted backwards from thirteen. She felt herself whirling upward, growing bigger and bigger by the second.

"Oh, good, it's working!" croaked Dorrie. She opened her eyes and looked at herself. "Oh, no! A GIANT TOAD! I've turned myself into a GIANT TOAD!"

Mr. Obs began jumping up and down inside the jar. He pointed at the Green Wizard. Dorrie looked. The Green Wizard was lifting the jar of Magic Elixir out of the cauldron.

"Oh, no you don't!" croaked Dorrie, opening her big toad mouth. Her long toad tongue flashed out, wrapped around the jar of Elixir and snatched it away from the Wizard. Reaching up, she tucked the jar into a bat cage hanging from the ceiling.

The Green Wizard tried to grab Dorrie. She stretched out one long leg and poked him in the stomach. Every time he came close, Dorrie poked him. He danced up and down with rage. Angrily muttering spells, he grabbed a stool and swung it at Dorrie.

She toppled over backwards with a plop, right on the floor.

The Wizard sprang up on the table. He reached up into the cage for the Magic Elixir. Down below Dorrie crouched, then leaped into the air toward the Wizard.

She sailed smack into the back of his knees. With a crash and a screech, the Wizard fell head over heels. He landed on the floor with a loud thud.

Dorrie peered over the edge of the table. The Green Wizard was lying very still. His eyes were shut. He was pale green. Mr. Obs jumped up and down inside the jar, clapping his toad hands and croaking, "Bravo, Dorrie! You saved us!"

Gink came out from behind a box and sniffed the Wizard's hat.

Dorrie hopped down from the table. "I need something to . . ."

Just then there was a knocking downstairs. Dorrie listened. She counted the knocks.

"Mother's home!"

Down, down, down the stairs went Dorrie, leaping three steps at a time. Gink went with her. Down the stairs, into the hall, to the front door they went. Dorrie reached up with her long fingers and pushed the latch back.

The door flew open. There was the Big Witch. Cook was right behind her. "Mother!" croaked Dorrie, throwing her long toad arms around her.

The Big Witch gasped, "Dorrie? Is that you, dear?"

"Quick!" croaked Dorrie. "The secret room. Before the Green Wizard wakes up and drinks all your Magic Elixir!"

Like a flash of black lightning, the Big Witch went up the stairs to the tower and into the secret room. Dorrie and Gink and Cook were right behind her.

Mr. Obs was hopping up and down, croaking, "Help! Stop, thief!" They were too late. The Green Wizard had leaped to the table. He grabbed the Elixir and drank it down before the Big Witch could blink.

"HA!" laughed the Green Wizard, pointing his finger at the Big Witch. "Now I've got you in my power at last! Your own Magic Elixir will protect me from your spells while I turn you into a TOAD, forever! And you, too, the fat one in the muffin hat!" he screeched, as Cook grabbed a bottle to throw at him.

The room suddenly grew very still. The Big Witch nodded toward the Green Wizard. They all watched. Something was happening to him.

He reached into his pouch for the Toad Powder Potion. He was moving very, very slowly. He slowly opened his mouth. "I . . . am . . . going . . . . to . . . . be . . . . . indestructible . . . . . for . . . . . ever . . . . and . . . . e . . v . . er . . . . r."

The Big Witch tapped him with her broomstick. "Hmmm," said the Big Witch, "he always did overdo things. Drinking the whole jar has made him so indestructible he's turned to stone!"

"Hmph!" scowled Cook. "Fat! Muffin hat! I'm going to go fix tea."

"Mother," said Dorrie, "I need your help to get Mr. Obs out of a jar."

When Mr. Obs was out, the Big Witch said, "Dear me, I must get busy on a recipe to un-toad you two." She looked through the pages of the *Book of Magic*. She frowned.

"The only recipe I can find takes hours to work," said the Big Witch.

"That's all right, Mother," croaked Dorrie. "I don't mind. Do you, Mr. Obs? We can have a tea party even if we are toads."

Mr. Obs smiled and clapped his toad hands together. "Tea for Toads, Toads for Tea! How delightful. I may commemorate the occasion with a violin solo. Later, of course."

"For a toad," croaked Dorrie, "you know a lot of big words!"

The Big Witch mixed up the recipe in the cauldron. Soon swirls of blue and green, puffs of purple, wisps of pink and red whirled around them. The Big Witch stirred and mumbled, mumbled and stirred. She lifted her hands in the air over Dorrie and Mr. Obs.

The sparks died away. The Big Witch clapped her hands. "There," she said. "I hope it works. And quickly. Having a toad call me 'Mother' is very upsetting."

A bell rang downstairs. "Teatime!" croaked Dorrie. Down, down, down the stairs they went and into the parlor.

Cook looked at them and frowned. "Toads in the parlor! Toads having tea! A green stone wizard in the tower!"

The Big Witch cut the fudge cake. "He's too big for a lamp. I know, we'll give him to the library. They've always wanted a statue for the garden."

Dorrie had some fudge cake. She gave Mr. Obs some fudge cake. Then she had some more. And a little more after that. And some watercress sandwiches. And more watercress sandwiches. And more fudge cake. And then there wasn't any more.

"Toads eat a lot," croaked Dorrie happily.

"I noticed," said the Big Witch. "And now it's bedtime."

Dorrie said goodnight. Up, up, up the stairs she went and Gink went with her. She had a bath with a lot of bubbles. She dried off with a big towel. With no teeth to brush and no hair to comb, it didn't take long to get ready.

Dorrie hopped into bed. Gink did, too. The Big Witch tucked Dorrie under the covers.

"Mother," croaked Dorrie, "I'm sorry the Wizard got your Elixir. Now you'll have to start all over."

The Big Witch smiled and gave Dorrie a kiss. "No, I won't. I've just learned something. A recipe like this brings more trouble than it keeps away."

Dorrie's eyes closed. The Big Witch looked at her. The toad face was changing. So were the fingers on the blanket. Soon there was no toad at all, it was just Dorrie herself asleep in bed.

Downstairs, Mr. Obs had turned back into himself, too. Even his violin was back. The Big Witch and Mr. Obs had a cup of tea together. Mr. Obs played a tune on his violin. He called it, "Two Toads at Teatime, or the Fudge Cake Fandango."